JUDITH S. SEIXAS

Junk Food -
WHAT IT IS,
WHAT IT DOES

Illustrated by
TOM HUFFMAN

GREENWILLOW BOOKS • New York

10 9 8 7 6 5 4

Library of Congress Cataloging in Publication Data
Seixas, Judith S.
Junk food—what it is, what it does.
(A Greenwillow read-alone book)
Summary: An introduction to facts about
junk food—what it is, where it is found,
and how it affects the body—with suggestions
for snacking more nutritionally.
   1. Food, Junk—Juvenile literature.
[I. Food, Junk.   2. Nutrition]
I. Huffman, Tom, ill.   II. Title.
III. Series: Greenwillow read-alone books.
TX370.S44   1984   641.1   83-14135
ISBN 0-688-02559-5
ISBN 0-688-02560-9 (lib. bdg.)

For Naomi Rebecca and Rachel Aviva,
who should enjoy as many years of
happy (healthy) eating as I have
   —J. S. S.

To Gregor—
who could use the information
in this book
   —T. H.

Contents

1. What Is Junk Food?

Junk food is food

that is high in calories

and low in nutrients.

Junk food may taste great.

It may be fun to eat.

But it will not help you grow.

It will not keep you healthy.

Have you ever seen a junkyard?

Junk is what people

throw away.

It is what they

do not need.

Junk food is food you do not need.
This book will help you find out
which foods are junk foods.
You will find out how much
junk food you have been eating,
and why too much junk food
is bad for you.

2. Facts You Should Know

Most people eat some junk food.

Small amounts of it are not harmful.

But if you eat junk food only

or large amounts of it, you may

 get sick easily

feel tired a lot

 not grow as tall as you would otherwise

grow too fat

 lose the shine in your hair

develop cavities in your teeth.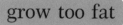

Junk food is low in nutrients.

The nutrients in food keep you well
and help you grow strong.
When you are sick,
nutrient-rich food will
help you get well.
Your body must have nutrients.

NUTRIENTS
carbohydrates
fats
proteins
minerals
vitamins
water

Touch the hood of a car
after a drive. It feels warm.
When a car engine runs,
it turns gas into heat and energy.
Touch your skin.
It too feels warm.
Your body runs like an engine.
It turns food into heat
and energy.
Like a car, you need a supply
of energy to move.
That supply is the food you eat.
You need it to walk, run, and play.
The energy you get from food
is measured in calories.

10

Junk food is high in calories.

Your body needs only a limited number of calories. The number you need depends on your weight and how active you are. If you eat too few calories, you will be too thin. If you eat too many calories, you will become overweight.

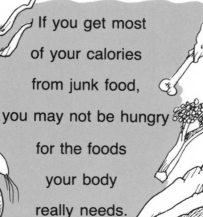

If you get most of your calories from junk food, you may not be hungry for the foods your body really needs.

3. The Foods Your Body Needs

Food Groups

The foods your body needs
are found in four food groups.

1. Fruits · vegetables

2. Grains breads cereals

3. Milk products

4. Fish · meat · beans · nuts · eggs

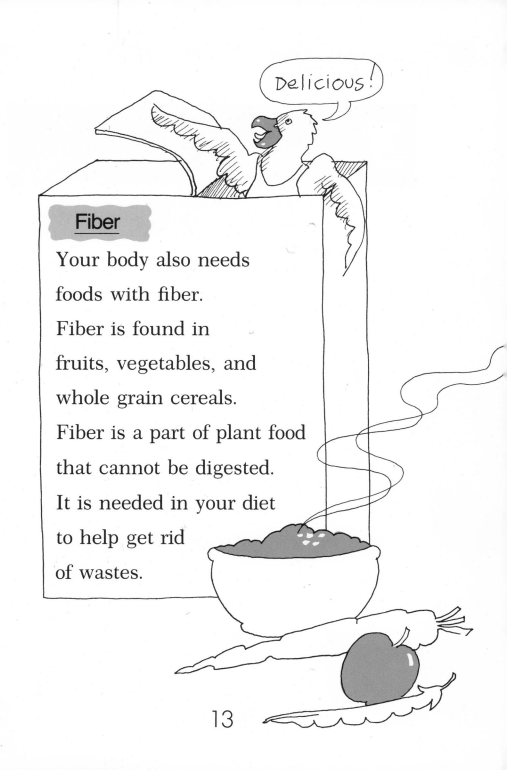

Fiber

Your body also needs
foods with fiber.
Fiber is found in
fruits, vegetables, and
whole grain cereals.
Fiber is a part of plant food
that cannot be digested.
It is needed in your diet
to help get rid
of wastes.

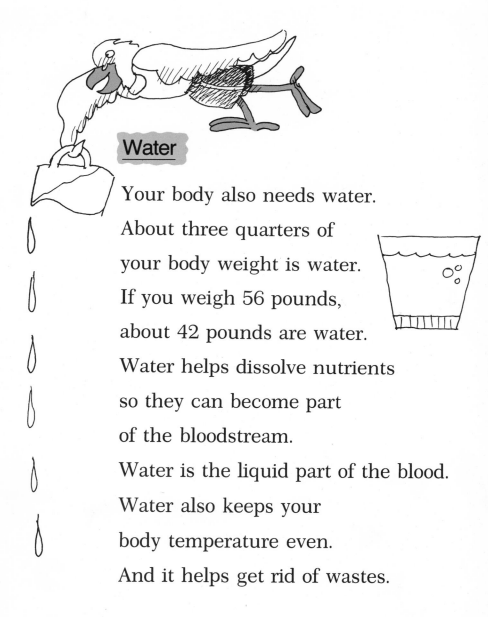

Water

Your body also needs water.
About three quarters of
your body weight is water.
If you weigh 56 pounds,
about 42 pounds are water.
Water helps dissolve nutrients
so they can become part
of the bloodstream.
Water is the liquid part of the blood.
Water also keeps your
body temperature even.
And it helps get rid of wastes.

A Balanced Diet

You can eat a lot and still get
too little of what your body needs.
To get enough nutrients and fiber,
you should eat a balanced diet.
A balanced diet must contain food
from each food group every day.
At your next meal,
look at the food on your plate.
The more colors you see,
the more likely it is that
you are eating a balanced diet.

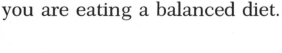

Here is an example of a good diet:
Orange juice, cereal,

and milk for breakfast.

A peanut butter sandwich, an apple,

and fruit juice for lunch.

Nuts for an afternoon snack.

Chicken, rice, peas, carrot sticks,

and oatmeal cookies for dinner.

If you eat this way most of the time,

your diet is balanced.

16

But if you eat a doughnut

for breakfast,

throw away most

of your school lunch,

snack on potato chips,

and pick at dinner,

you are not eating

the way you should.

17

4. How Your Body Works

The food you swallow is turned into blood, fat, bone, muscle, hair, nails, skin, teeth, and body organs.

18

Here is how it happens:

. . . you take a bite of food

. . . it mixes with saliva

. . . you swallow it

. . . it travels slowly through your body

. . . as it travels, it is broken down
into smaller and smaller bits

. . . they mix with oxygen
and other chemicals

. . . new chemicals are formed

. . . these mix with your blood

. . . your blood carries them
to all parts of your body.

The parts of food your body

does not use come out in waste.

Liquid wastes are urine.

Solid wastes are bowel movements.

5. The Tempters—Sugar, Fat, Salt

Too much sugar in your diet
is harmful.
Years ago people ate about
two pounds of sugar a year.
Now many people eat that much
every week.

20

Today sugar-filled junk food
is everywhere you look—
in vending machines,
at candy counters,
and in supermarkets.
It is also in our homes.
TV ads constantly tell us
to buy these foods.
Some experts say sugar
is habit-forming.
The more sugar you eat,
the more you will want.
Now is the time to cut down—
before you have the sugar habit.

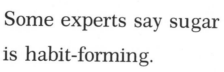

Sugar is bad for your teeth.
The bacteria that live in
your mouth feed on sugar.
They turn it into acid.
Acid causes tooth decay.
When you eat sugar,
get it out of your mouth fast!
The longer it stays,
the more damage it can do.

WE LOVE IT!

Do not suck on hard candy
for hours at a time.
Brush your teeth after you eat.
If you can't, then rinse your mouth.
Do not go to bed with anything
sweet in your mouth.
Always brush your teeth
before you go to bed.

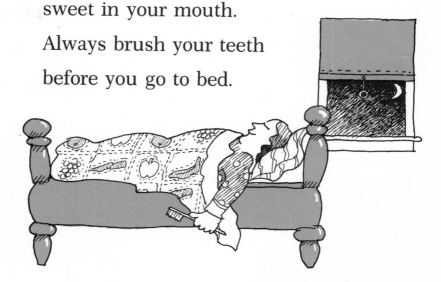

Fat

Everyone needs some fat.

It is the nutrient highest in calories.

Your body stores fat.

Some is used for energy.

Some forms a layer under your skin.

It keeps heat in and cold out.

It also cushions parts of your body.

It even cushions the soles of your feet.

And it forms a cushion to sit on.

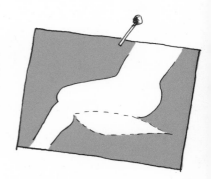

When you grow older, too much fat
may lead to trouble with breathing,
exercising, and even walking.
It may lead to serious health problems.

The high fat foods most kids like
are corn chips and potato chips,
baloney, hot dogs, doughnuts,
ice cream, mayonnaise,
and anything fried.

Salt

Test your body for salt.
All you have to do
is lick your arm.
Does it taste salty?
Small amounts of salt come
out of your body all the time.
Salt comes out in tears and urine.
It also comes out in perspiration.
On hot days or when you
exercise a lot,
you will lose more salt.
So it always needs to be replaced.

Most of the time salt is replaced
by what you eat.
You do not have to add extra salt.
People who get used to salty food
find it hard to cut down on it.
As you get older,
too much salt can be harmful.
Doctors say that too much salt
is a cause of high blood pressure.
High blood pressure often leads
to heart disease.

Leave the
shaker off
the table.

27

6. Additives

Many foods contain additives.
Sometimes vitamins and minerals
are added to food.
They are good for you.
They are used to fortify milk
and to enrich bread.
Other additives are used to
- - - . keep food tasting and looking fresh
- - - . make food stay creamy or crisp
- - - . keep fats and oils from turning sour
- - - . make the color of food more attractive.

28

By law most food packages
must have labels.
The labels list the number
of calories in the food.
They must also list
all the ingredients.

Read food labels.

The longer the list,
the more additives in the food.
Some may be bad for you.
Experts don't always agree
on which ones are harmful.

7. Snack Time—

Eating and Drinking Junk

What will you choose?

It's a good idea to have a snack
when you're hungry or thirsty.
It's not a good idea to fill up
on junk food snacks.
You will not have room for
the foods your body needs.

Solid snacks

Good snacks contain nutrients and fiber. They do not have too much sugar, fat, or salt. They do not have harmful additives. Fruits, nuts, seeds, eggs, bread and peanut butter, and raw vegetables are good snacks.

The solid snacks kids most often have are candy bars, chips, fries, packaged cakes, and doughnuts. These are junk snacks.

31

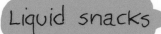

Liquid snacks

Milk is the best snack
unless you are allergic to it.
Milk is full of nutrients.
A shake consists of milk,
sugar, and flavoring.
Ice cream makes it a thick shake.

Sometimes additives are used
to make a thick shake even thicker.
Shakes with additives
are junk drinks.

Fresh fruit juices are good for you.
When you drink frozen,
canned, or bottled juices,
read the label first.
If it says, "Pure juice . . .
no additives or preservatives,"
you will not be drinking junk.

The liquid snacks most kids have
are shakes with additives,
imitation fruit drinks, soda or pop,
or packaged drink mixes.
These are junk drinks.

Imitation fruit drinks
are mostly sugar and water.
Flavors and colors are added.
They have very little pure
fruit juice in them.
Soda and other soft drinks
are also mostly sugar and water.
Caffeine is sometimes added.
Caffeine is a drug you do not need.

34

Packaged drink mixes
start as sugary powders.
They come in bright colors,
like purple or green.
You add water.
Chemicals make them
taste like fruit.

Some junk drinks have no sugar.
They are "artificially sweetened"
with chemical additives.

What about...

SUGAR-COATED CEREAL

It is half cereal
and half sugar.
Don't be fooled
by fancy colors.
Unsweetened cereals
are better for you.

WHITE BREAD

It is made from bleached flour
from which the germ
and bran have been removed.
Most of the nutrients in flour are
found in the germ and bran.
The best bread is bread
made of *whole grain* flour.

POPCORN

It is corn.

It is a healthy food.

But butter-flavored oil

is often added.

So is salt.

These make it

a junk food.

FRENCH FRIED POTATOES
AND POTATO CHIPS

They are cooked at high heat.

High heat cooks out nutrients.

Fats and salt are added.

Then good potatoes

become junk potatoes.

CHOCOLATE CANDY

It has oils and caffeine in it.
But it is mostly sugar.
One small candy bar has
about the same amount
of sugar as fifteen apples!

CALORIE	AND
FOOD	
	A 2 OUNCE BAG OF ARTIFICIALLY FLAVORED POTATO CHIPS
	A SINGLE SCOOP ICE CREAM CONE
	A 12 OUNCE CAN OF SODA
	A CUP OF PLAIN YOGURT
	¼ CUP OF RAISINS
	AN 8 OUNCE GLASS OF LOWFAT MILK
	AN ORANGE
	A CARROT

ICE CREAM

It has many nutrients.
But it is full of sugar and fats.
Enjoy it now and then.

NUTRIENT CHART	
CALORIES	NUTRIENTS
340	HARDLY ANY
300	HIGH IN NUTRIENTS HIGH IN FATS
300	HARDLY ANY
150	HIGH IN NUTRIENTS
100	HIGH IN NUTRIENTS
90	HIGH IN NUTRIENTS
75	HIGH IN NUTRIENTS HIGH IN FIBER AND VITAMIN C
30	HIGH IN NUTRIENTS HIGH IN FIBER AND VITAMIN A

Junk Food Quiz:

How much junk food do you eat?

- Do you eat candy nearly every day?
- Do you drink soda nearly every day?
- Are the cereals you eat coated with sugar?
- Are your sandwiches always made of white bread?
- Do you always have cake or cookies for dessert?
- Do you snack on sweets or chips?
- Do you add salt to your food even before you taste it?
- Do you eat a lot of fried foods?

40

If you have *four*
or more YES answers,
you are on your way
to a junk food habit.
Now you may want
to check what you eat
before you eat it.

If you have eight YES
answers, you have a junk
food habit.

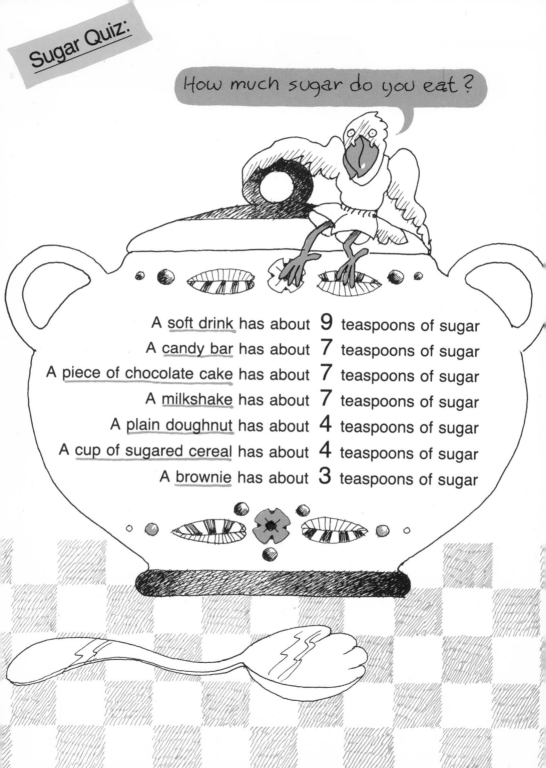

It is best to eat less than 13 teaspoons of sugar a day.

Can you remember
what you ate yesterday?
Add up the teaspoons of sugar.
Did you eat more than 13?
If you find out that you are eating
too much sugar, you can cut down.
You may then be surprised.
Many foods will taste sweeter to you.

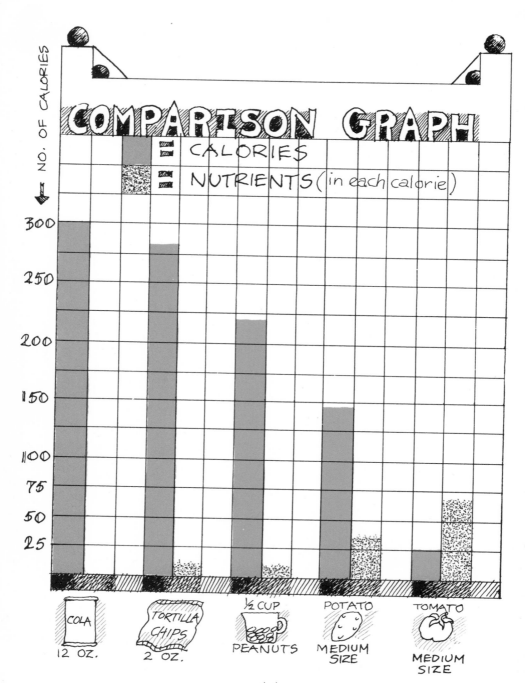

NO. OF CALORIES

COMPARISON GRAPH

█ = CALORIES
▒ = NUTRIENTS (in each calorie)

300
250
200
150
100
75
50
25

COLA
12 OZ.

TORTILLA CHIPS
2 OZ.

½ CUP
PEANUTS

POTATO
MEDIUM SIZE

TOMATO
MEDIUM SIZE

9. You Can Choose

There is no question about it.

Junk food tastes good.

Many kids will "pig out" on it.

But now you know more about

good food and junk food.

You know the problems

you can have if you eat

too much junk food.

Your food choices can be based

on the facts you know.

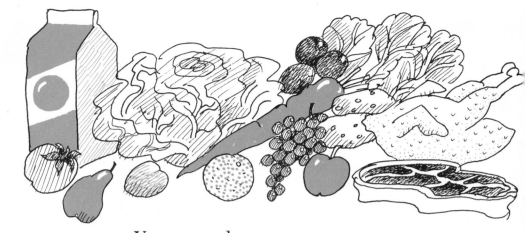

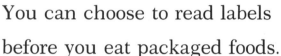

You can choose to eat
a balanced diet and you now
know what a balanced diet is.
You can choose to read labels
before you eat packaged foods.
You can choose snacks high in nutrients
instead of eating those additive- and
sugar-filled snacks advertised on TV.
You can steer away from "the tempters."

Most kids don't think a lot
about what they eat.
They think they will grow strong
and stay healthy no matter
what they eat.
But now you know what junk food
is and what junk food does.
You can choose the foods
that not only taste good
but are the best for you.

JUDITH S. SEIXAS has long been involved in health issues, specializing in the treatment of alcoholics and their families. Her wide experience encompasses both the educational and the therapeutic. She is a Certified Alcoholism Counselor in New York State and is now working with adult children of alcoholics in the Boston area.

Mrs. Seixas was graduated from Carleton College and has an M.A. from Columbia's Teachers College. She also has a certificate from the Rutgers Summer School of Alcohol Studies. She is the author of *Tobacco—What It Is, What It Does*, *Alcohol—What It Is, What It Does*, and *Living with a Parent Who Drinks Too Much*.

TOM HUFFMAN attended the School of Visual Arts in New York City and holds a B.A. from the University of Kentucky. Mr. Huffman is a free-lance artist whose drawings have appeared in national magazines. He has illustrated many children's books, including four Greenwillow Read-alone Books (*Alcohol—What It Is, What It Does, Exercise—What It Is, What It Does, Tobacco—What It Is, What It Does*, and *Pot—What It Is, What It Does*), as well as many other children's books, including *Santa Rat* and *America's Very Own Monsters.*